Hamilton Wright Mabie, Will Hicok Low

In the forest of Arden

Hamilton Wright Mabie, Will Hicok Low

In the forest of Arden

ISBN/EAN: 9783743367890

Manufactured in Europe, USA, Canada, Australia, Japa

Cover: Foto ©Andreas Hilbeck / pixelio.de

Manufactured and distributed by brebook publishing software
(www.brebook.com)

Hamilton Wright Mabie, Will Hicok Low

In the forest of Arden

IN THE FOREST OF ARDEN

TO ARDEN

BY
HAMILTON
WRIGHT
MABIE

DECORATED
BY
WILL H LOW

NEW YORK PUBLISHED BY DODD MEAD AND COMPANY MDCCCXCIX

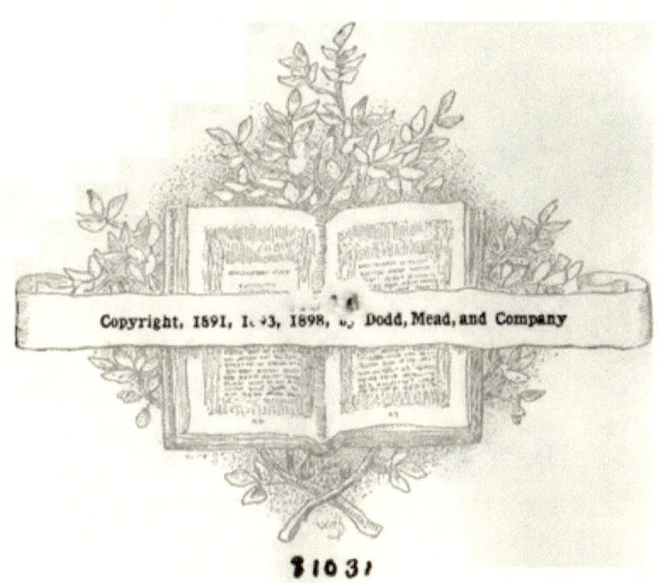

81031

The University Press, Cambridge, U. S. A.

In the Forest of Arden

Go with me: if you like, upon report,
The soil, the profit, and this kind of life,
I will your very faithful factor be,
And buy it with your gold right suddenly

TO MY SISTER

"AND I FOR ROSALIND"

I

Under the greenwood tree,
Who loves to lie with me,
And turn his merry note
Unto the sweet bird's throat,
Come hither, come hither, come hither

Rosalind had just laid a spray of apple blossoms on the study table.

"Well," I said, "when shall we start?"

"To-morrow."

Rosalind has a habit of swift decision when she has settled a question in her own mind, and I was not surprised when she replied with a single decisive word. But she also has a habit of making thorough preparation for any undertaking, and now she was quietly proposing to go off for the summer the very next day, and not a trunk was packed, not a seat secured in any train, not a movement made toward any winding up of household affairs. I had great faith in her ability to execute her plans with celerity, but I doubted whether she could be ready to turn the key in the door, bid farewell to the milkman and the butcher, and start the very next day

3

for the Forest of Arden. For several past seasons we had planned this bold excursion into a country which few persons have seemed to know much about since the day when a poet of great fame, familiar with many strange climes and peoples, found his way thither and shared the golden fortune of his journey with all the world. Winter after winter, before the study fire, we had made merry plans for this trip into the magical forest; we had discussed the best methods of travelling where no roads led; we had enjoyed in anticipation the surmises of our neighbours concerning our unexplained absence, and the delightful mystery which would always linger about us when we had returned, with memories of a landscape which no eyes but ours had seen these many years, and of rare and original people whose voices had been silent in common speech so

4

many generations that only a few dreamers like ourselves even remembered that they had ever spoken. We had looked along the library shelves for the books we should take with us, until we remembered that in that country there were books in the running streams. Rosalind had gone so far as to lay aside a certain volume of sermons whose aspiring note had more than once made music of the momentary discords of her life; but I reminded her that such a work would be strangely out of place in a forest where there were sermons in stones. Finally we had decided to leave books behind and go free-minded as well as free-hearted. It had been a serious question how much and what apparel we should take with us, and that point was still unsettled when the apple trees came to their blossoming. It is a theory of mine that the chief delight of a vacation from one's

5

usual occupations is freedom from the tyranny of plans and dates, and thus much Rosalind had conceded to me.

There had been an irresistible charm in the very secrecy which protected our adventure from the curious and unsympathetic comment of the world. We found endless pleasure in imagining what this and that good neighbour of ours would say about the folly of leaving a comfortable house, good beds, and a well-stocked larder for the hard fare and uncertain shelter of a strange forest. "For my part," we gleefully heard Mrs. Grundy declare, — "for my part, I cannot understand why two people old enough to know better should make tramps of themselves and go rambling about a piece of woods that nobody ever heard of, in the heat of the midsummer." Poor Mrs. Grundy! We could well afford to laugh merrily at her scornful expostulations; for while she was repeating platitudes to over-dressed and uninteresting people at Old-port, we should be making sunny play of life with men and women whose thoughts were free as the wind, and whose hearts were fresh as the dew and the stars. And often when our talk had died into silence, and the wind with-out whistled to the fire within, we had fallen to dreaming of those shadowy aisles arched by the mighty trees, and of the splendid pageant that should make life seem as great and rich as Nature herself. I confess that all my dreams came to one ending; that I should suddenly awake in some golden hour and really know Rosalind. Of course I had been coming, through all these years, to know something about Rosalind; but in this busy world, with work to be done, and bills to be paid, and people to be seen, and journeys to be made, and friction and worry and fatigue to be borne, how can we really come to know one another? We may meet the vicissitudes and changes side by side; we may work together in the long days of toil; our hearts may repose on a common trust, our thoughts travel a common road; but how rarely do we come to the hour when the pressure of toil is removed, the clouds of anxiety melt into blue sky, and in the whole world nothing remains but the sun on the flower, and the song in the trees, and the unclouded light of love in the eyes?

I dreamed, too, that in finding Rosalind I should also find myself. There were times when I had seemed on the very point of making this discovery, but something had always turned me aside when the quest was most eager and promising; the world pressed into the seclusion for which I had struggled, and when I waited to hear its faintest murmur die in the distance, suddenly the tumult had risen again, and the dream of self-communion and self-knowledge had vanished. To get out of the uproar and confusion of things, I had often fancied, would be like exchanging the dusty mid-summer road for the shade of the woods where the brook calms the day with its pellucid note of effortless flow, and the hours hide themselves from the glances of the sun. In the Forest of Arden I felt sure I should find the repose, the quietude, the freedom of thought, which would permit me to know myself. There, too, I suspected Nature had certain surprises for me; certain secrets which she has been holding back for the fortunate hour when her spell would be supreme and unbroken. I even hoped that I might come unaware upon that ancient and perennial movement of life upon which I seemed

9

always to happen the very second after it had been suspended; that I might hear the note of the hermit thrush breaking out of the heart of the forest; the soulful melody of the nightingale, pathetic with unappeasable sorrow. In the Forest of Arden, too, there were unspoiled men and women, as indifferent to the fashion of the world and the folly of the hour as the stars to the impalpable mist of the clouds; men and women who spoke the truth, and saw the fact, and lived the right; to whom love and faith and high hopes were more real than the crowns of which they had been despoiled, and the kingdoms from which they had been rejected. All this I had dreamed, and I know not how many other brave and beautiful dreams, and I was dreaming them again when Rosalind laid the apple blossoms on the study table, and answered, decisively, "To-morrow."

"To-morrow," I repeated, "to-morrow. But how are you going to get ready? If you sit up all night you cannot get through with the packing. You said only yesterday that your summer dressmaking was shamefully behind. My dear, next week is the earliest possible time for our going."

Rosalind laughed archly, and pushed the apple blossoms over the wofully interlined manuscript of my new article on Egypt. There was in her very attitude a hint of unsuspected buoyancy and strength; there was in her eyes a light which I have never seen under our uncertain skies. The breath of the apple blossoms filled the room, and a bobolink, poised on a branch outside the window, suddenly poured a rapturous song into the silence of the sweet spring day. I laid down my pen, pushed my scattered sheets into

the portfolio, covered the inkstand, and laid my hand in hers. "Not to-morrow," I said, "not to-morrow. Let us go now."

II

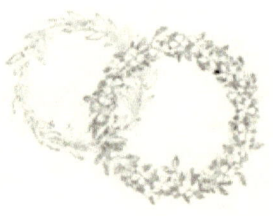

Now go we in content
To liberty and not to banishment

I have sometimes entertained myself
by trying to imagine the impressions
which our modern life would make
upon some sensitive mind of a remote
age. I have fancied myself rambling
about New York with Montaigne,
and taking note of his shrewd, satirical
comment. I can hardly imagine him
expressing any feeling of surprise, much
less any sentiment of admiration; but
I am confident that under a masque of
ironical self-complacency the old Gascon
would find it difficult to repress his
astonishment, and still more difficult to
adjust his mind to evident and impres-
sive changes. I have ventured at times
to imagine myself in the company of
another more remote and finely organ-
ised spirit of the past, and pictured to
myself the keen, dispassionate criticism of
Pericles on the things of modern habit
and creation; I have listened to his
luminous interpretations of the changed

conditions which he saw about him; I have noted his unconcern toward the merely material advances of society, his penetrative insight into its intellectual and moral developments. A mind so capacious and open, a nature so trained and poised, could not be otherwise than self-contained and calm even in the presence of changes so vast and manifold as those which have transformed society since the days of the great Athenian; but even he could not be quite unmoved if brought face to face with a life so unlike that with which he had been familiar; there must come, even to one who feels the mastery of the soul over all conditions, a certain sense of wonder and awe.

It was with some such feeling that Rosalind and I found ourselves in the Forest of Arden. The journey was so soon accomplished that we had no time

to accustom ourselves to the changes
between the country we had left and
that to which we had come. We had
always fancied that the road would be
long and hard, and that we should
arrive worn and spent with the fatigues
of travel. We were astonished and delighted when we suddenly discovered
that we were within the boundaries of
the Forest long before we had begun
to think of the end of our journey. We
had said nothing to each other by the
way; our thoughts were so busy that
we had no time for speech. There were
no other travellers; everybody seemed
to be going in the opposite direction;
and we were left to undisturbed medi-
tation. The route to the Forest is one
of those open secrets which whosoever
would know must learn for himself; it
is impossible to direct those who do not
discover for themselves how to make
the journey. The Forest is probably

the most accessible place on the face of the earth, but it is so rarely visited that one may go half a lifetime without meeting a person who has been there. I have never been able to explain the fact that those who have spent some time in the Forest, as well as those who are later to see it, seem to recognise each other by instinct. Rosalind and I happen to have a large circle of acquaintances, and it has been our good fortune to meet and recognise many who were familiar with the Forest, and who were able to tell us much about its localities and charms. It is not generally known, and it is probably wise not to emphasise the fact, that the fortunate few who have access to the Forest form a kind of secret fraternity; a brotherhood of the soul which is secret because those alone who are qualified for membership by nature can understand either its language or its aims. It is a very strange thing that the dwellers in the Forest never make the least attempt at concealment, but that, no matter how frank and explicit their statements may be, nobody outside the brotherhood ever understands where the Forest lies, or what one finds when he gets there. One may write what he chooses about life in the Forest, and only those whom Nature has selected and trained will understand what he discloses; to all others it will be an idle tale or a fairy story for the entertainment of people who have no serious business in hand.

I remember well the first time I ever understood that there is a Forest of Arden, and that they who choose may wander through its arched aisles of shade and live at their will in its deep and beautiful solitude; a solitude in which nature sits like a friend from whose face the veil has been with-

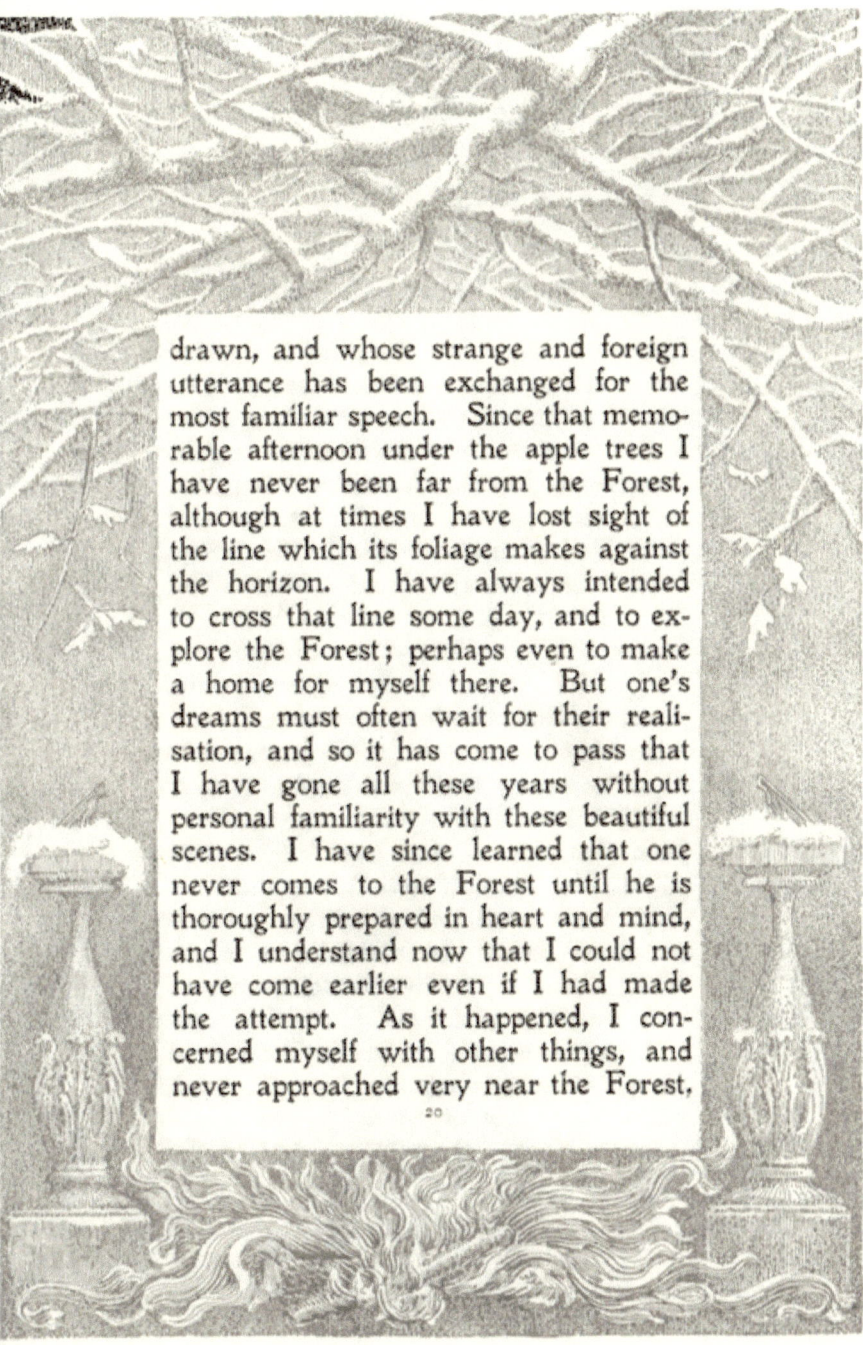

drawn, and whose strange and foreign utterance has been exchanged for the most familiar speech. Since that memorable afternoon under the apple trees I have never been far from the Forest, although at times I have lost sight of the line which its foliage makes against the horizon. I have always intended to cross that line some day, and to explore the Forest; perhaps even to make a home for myself there. But one's dreams must often wait for their realisation, and so it has come to pass that I have gone all these years without personal familiarity with these beautiful scenes. I have since learned that one never comes to the Forest until he is thoroughly prepared in heart and mind, and I understand now that I could not have come earlier even if I had made the attempt. As it happened, I concerned myself with other things, and never approached very near the Forest, although never very far from it. I was never quite happy unless I caught frequent glimpses of its distant boughs, and I searched more and more eagerly for those who had left some record of their journeys to the Forest, and of their life within its magical boundaries. I discovered, to my great joy, that the libraries were full of books which had much to say about the delights of Arden: its enchanting scenery; the music of its brooks; the sweet and refreshing repose of its recesses; the noble company that frequent it. I soon found that all the greater poets have been there, and that their lines had caught the magical radiance of the sky; and many of the prose writers showed the same familiarity with a country in which they evidently found whatever was sweetest and best in life. I came to know at last those whose knowledge of Arden was most complete, and I put

them in a place by themselves; a cor-
ner in the study to which Rosalind
and I went for the books we read together. I would gladly give a list of
these works but for the fact I have
already hinted — that those who would
understand their references to Arden
will come to know them without aid
from me, and that those who would
not understand could find nothing in
them even if I should give page and
paragraph. It was a great surprise to
me, when I first began to speak of the
Forest, to find that most people scouted
the very idea of such a country; many
did not even understand what I meant.
Many a time, at sunset, when the light
has lain soft and tender on the distant
Forest, I have pointed it out, only to be
told that what I thought was the Forest
was a splendid pile of clouds, a shining
mass of mist. I came to understand at
last that Arden exists only for a few,

and I ceased to talk about it save to those who shared my faith. Gradually I came to number among my friends many who were in the habit of making frequent journeys to the Forest, and not a few who had spent the greater part of their lives there. I remember the first time I saw Rosalind I saw the light of the Arden sky in her eyes, the buoyancy of the Arden air in her step, the purity and freedom of the Arden life in her nature. We built our home within sight of the Forest, and there was never a day that we did not talk about and plan our long-delayed journey thither.

"After all," said Rosalind, on that first glorious morning in Arden, "as I look back I see that we were always on the way here."

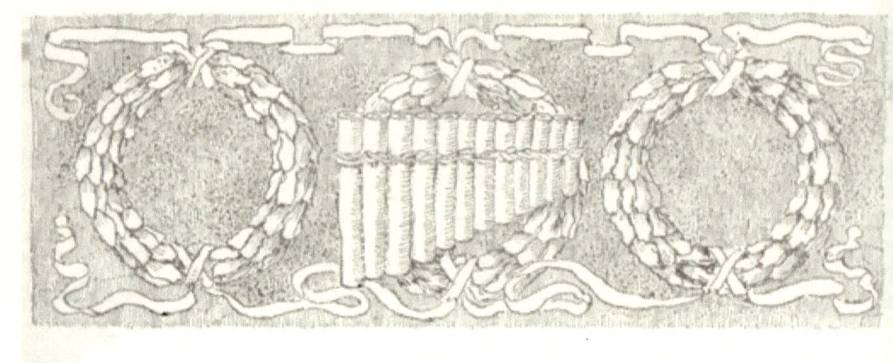

III

Well, this is the Forest of Arden

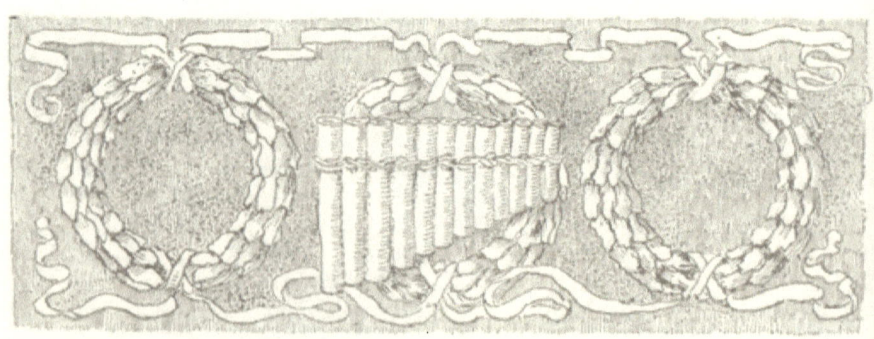

The first sensation that comes to one who finds himself at last within the boundaries of the Forest of Arden is a delicious sense of freedom. I am not sure that there is not a certain sympathy with outlawry in that first exhilarating consciousness of having gotten out of the conventional world, —the world whose chief purpose is that all men shall wear the same coat, eat the same dinner, repeat the same polite commonplaces, and be forgotten at last under the same epitaph. Forests have been the natural refuge of outlaws from the earliest time, and among the most respectable persons there has always been an ill-concealed liking for Robin Hood and the whole fraternity of the men of the bow. Truth is above all things characteristic of the dwellers in Arden, and it must be frankly confessed at the beginning, therefore, that the Forest is given over entirely to outlaws; those who have committed some grave offence against the world of conventions, or who have voluntarily gone into exile out of sheer liking for a freer life. These persons are not vulgar law-breakers; they have neither blood on their hands nor ill-gotten gains in their pockets; they are, on the contrary, people of uncommonly honest bearing and frank speech. Their offences evidently impose small burden on their conscience, and they have the air of those who have never known what it is to have the Furies on one's track. Rosalind was struck with the charming naturalness and gaiety of every one we met in our first ramble on that delicious and never-to-be-forgotten morning when we arrived in Arden. There was neither assumption nor diffidence; there was rather an entire absence of any kind of self-consciousness. Rosalind had fancied that we might be quite

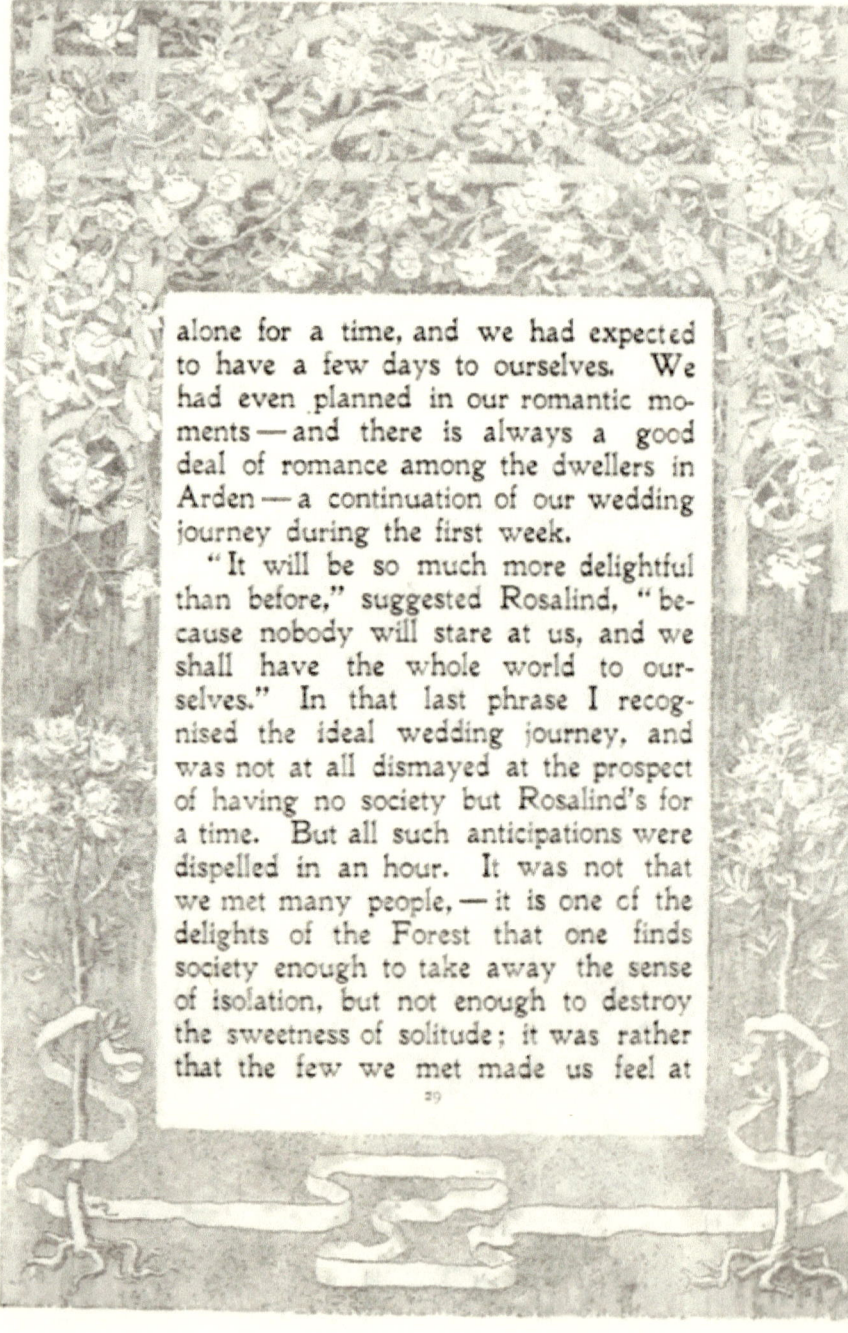

alone for a time, and we had expected
to have a few days to ourselves. We
had even planned in our romantic moments — and there is always a good
deal of romance among the dwellers in
Arden — a continuation of our wedding
journey during the first week.

"It will be so much more delightful
than before," suggested Rosalind, "because nobody will stare at us, and we
shall have the whole world to ourselves." In that last phrase I recognised the ideal wedding journey, and
was not at all dismayed at the prospect
of having no society but Rosalind's for
a time. But all such anticipations were
dispelled in an hour. It was not that
we met many people, — it is one of the
delights of the Forest that one finds
society enough to take away the sense
of isolation, but not enough to destroy
the sweetness of solitude; it was rather
that the few we met made us feel at

once that we had equal claim with themselves on the hospitality of the place. The Forest was not only free to every comer, but it evidently gave peculiar pleasure to those who were living in it to convey a sense of owner- ship to those who were arriving for the first time. Rosalind declared that she felt as much at home as if she had been born there; and she added that she was glad she had brought only the dress she wore. I was a little puzzled by the last remark; it seemed not entirely logical. But I saw presently that she was expressing the fellowship of the place, which for- bade that one should possess anything that was not in use, and that, there- fore, was not adding constantly to the common stock of pleasure. Concerning the feeling of having been born in Arden, I became convinced later that there was good reason for believing

that everybody who loved the place
had been born there, and that this fact
explained the home feeling which came
to one the instant he set foot within
the Forest. It is, in fact, the only place
I have known which seemed to belong
to me and to everybody else at the
same time; in which I felt no alien
influence. In our own home I had
something of the same feeling, but
when I looked from a window or set
foot from a door I was instantly op-
pressed with a sense of foreign ownership. In the great world how little
could I call my own! Only a few
feet of soil out of the measureless landscape; only a few trees and flowers
out of all that boundless foliage! I
seemed driven out of the heritage to
which I was born; cheated out of my
birthright in the beauty of the field and
the mystery of the Forest; put off with
the beggarly portion of a younger son

when I ought to have fallen heir to the kingdom. My chief joy was that from the little space I called my own I could see the whole heavens; no man could rob me of that splendid vision.

In Arden, however, the question of ownership never comes into one's thoughts; that the Forest belongs to you gives you a deep joy, but there is a deeper joy in the consciousness that it belongs to everybody else.

The sense of freedom, which comes as strongly to one in Arden as the smell of the sea to one who has made a long journey from the inland, hints, I suppose, at the offence which makes the dwellers within its boundaries outlaws. For one reason or another, they have all revolted against the rule of the world, and the world has cast them out. They have offended smug respectability, with its passionless de-

votion to deportment; they have out-
raged conventional usage, that carefully
devised system by which small natures
attempt to bring great ones down to
their own dimensions; they have scan-
dalised the orthodoxy which, like Mem-
non, has lost the music of its morning,
and marvels that the world no longer
listens; they have derided venerable
prejudices, — those ugly relics by which
some men keep in remembrance their
barbarous ancestry; they have refused
to follow flags whose battles were won
or lost ages ago; they have scorned to
compromise with untruth, to go with
the crowd, to acquiesce in evil "for the
good of the cause," to speak when they
ought to keep silent, and to keep silent
when they ought to speak. Truly the
lists of sins charged to the account of
Arden is a long one, and were it not
that the memory of the world, concerned
chiefly with the things that make for

its comfort, is a short one, it would go ill with the lovers of the Forest. More than once it has happened that some offender has suffered so long a banishment that he has taken permanent refuge in Arden, and proved his citizenship there by some act worthy of its glorious privileges. In the Forest one comes constantly upon traces of those who, like Dante and Milton, have found there a refuge from the Philistinism of a world that often hates its children in exact proportion to their ability to give it light. For the most part, however, the outlaws who frequent the Forest suffer no longer banishment than that which they impose on themselves. They come and go at their own sweet will; and their coming, I suspect, is generally a matter of their own choosing. The world still loves darkness more than light; but it rarely nowadays falls upon the lantern-bearer

34

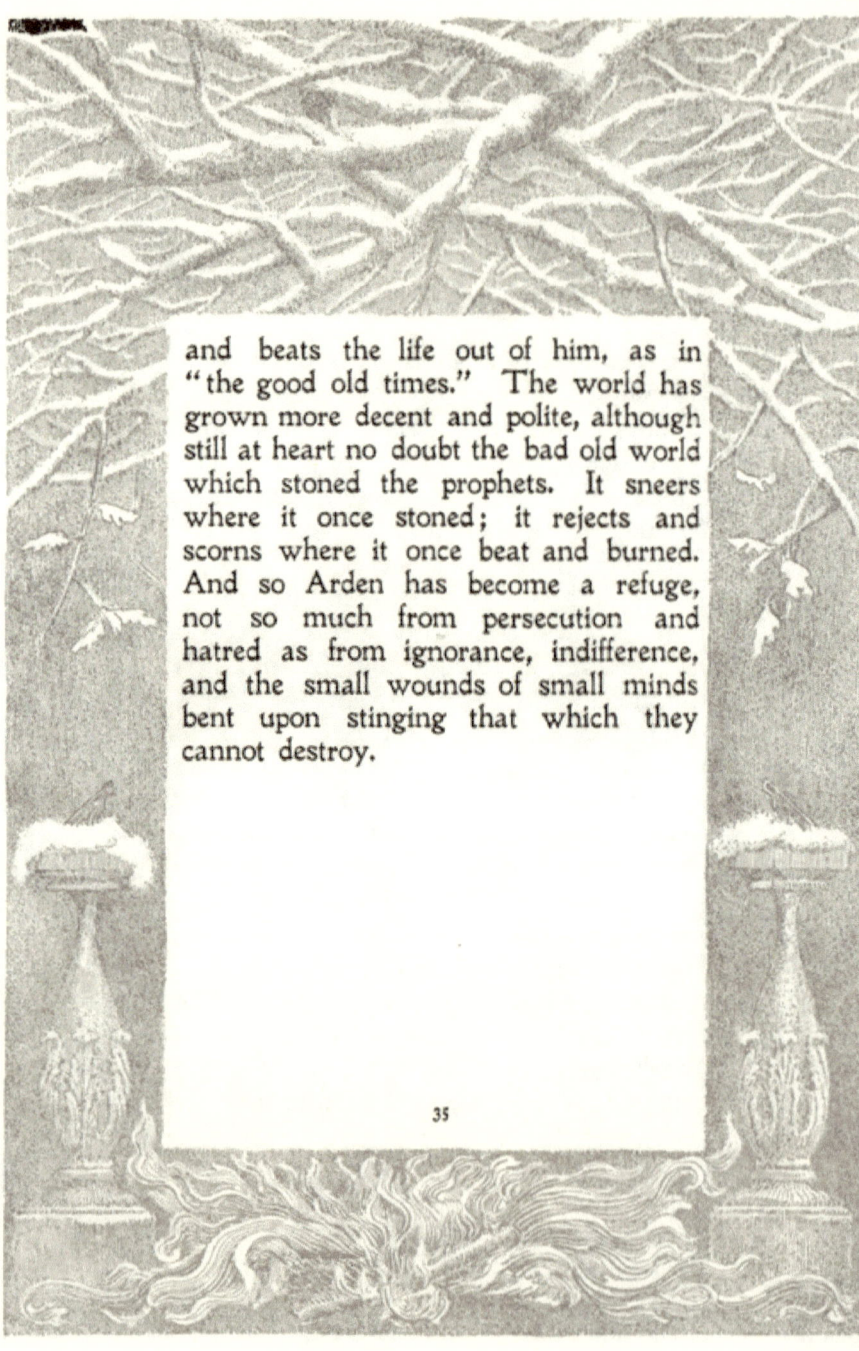

and beats the life out of him, as in "the good old times." The world has grown more decent and polite, although still at heart no doubt the bad old world which stoned the prophets. It sneers where it once stoned; it rejects and scorns where it once beat and burned. And so Arden has become a refuge, not so much from persecution and hatred as from ignorance, indifference, and the small wounds of small minds bent upon stinging that which they cannot destroy.

35

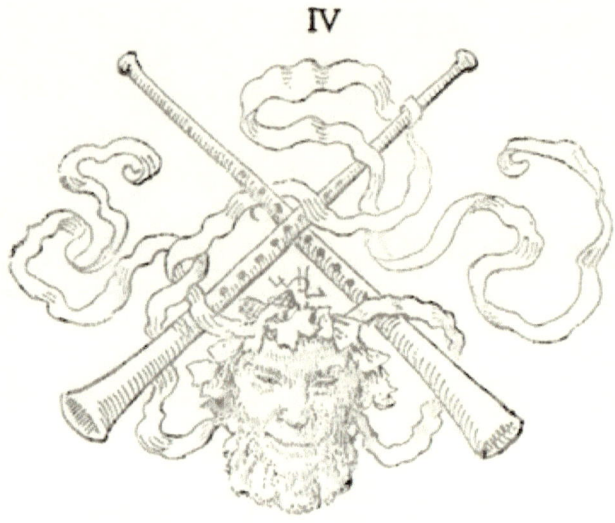

IV

... Fleet the time carelessly, as they did in the golden world

Rosalind and I have always been planning to do a great many pleasant things when we had more time. During the busy days when we barely found opportunity to speak to each other we were always thinking of the better days when we should be able to sit hours together with no knock at the door and no imperative summons from the kitchen. Some man of sufficient eminence to give his words currency ought to define life as a series of interruptions. There are a good many valuable and inspiring things which can only be done when one is in the mood, and to secure a mood is not always an easy matter; there are moods which are as coy as the most high-spirited woman, and must be wooed with as much patience and tact: and when the illusive prize is gained, one holds it by the frailest tenure. An interruption diverts the current, cuts the golden thread, breaks the exquisite harmony. I have often thought that Dante was far less unfortunate than the world has judged him to be. If he had been courted and crowned instead of rejected and exiled, it might have been that his genius would have missed the conditions which gave it immortal utterance. Left to himself, he had only his own nature to reckon with; the world passed him by, and left him to the companionship of his sublime and awful dreams. To be left alone with one's self is often the highest good fortune. Moreover, I detest being hurried; it seems to me the most offensive way in which we are reminded of our mortality; there is time enough if we know how to use it. People who, like Goethe, never rest and never haste, complete their work and escape the friction of it.

One of the most delightful things

about life in Arden is the absence of any sense of haste; life is a matter of being rather than of doing, and one shares the tranquillity of the great trees that silently expand year by year. The fever and restlessness are gone, the long strain of nerve and will relaxed; a delicious feeling of having strength and time enough to live one's life and do one's work fills one with a deep and enduring sense of repose.

Rosalind, who had been busy about so many things that I sometimes almost lost sight of her for days together, found time to take long walks with me, to watch the birds and the clouds, and talk by the hour about all manner of pleasant trifles. I came to feel, after a time, that just what I anticipated would happen in Arden had happened. I was fast becoming acquainted with her. We spent days together in the most delightful half-vocal and half-silent fellowship:

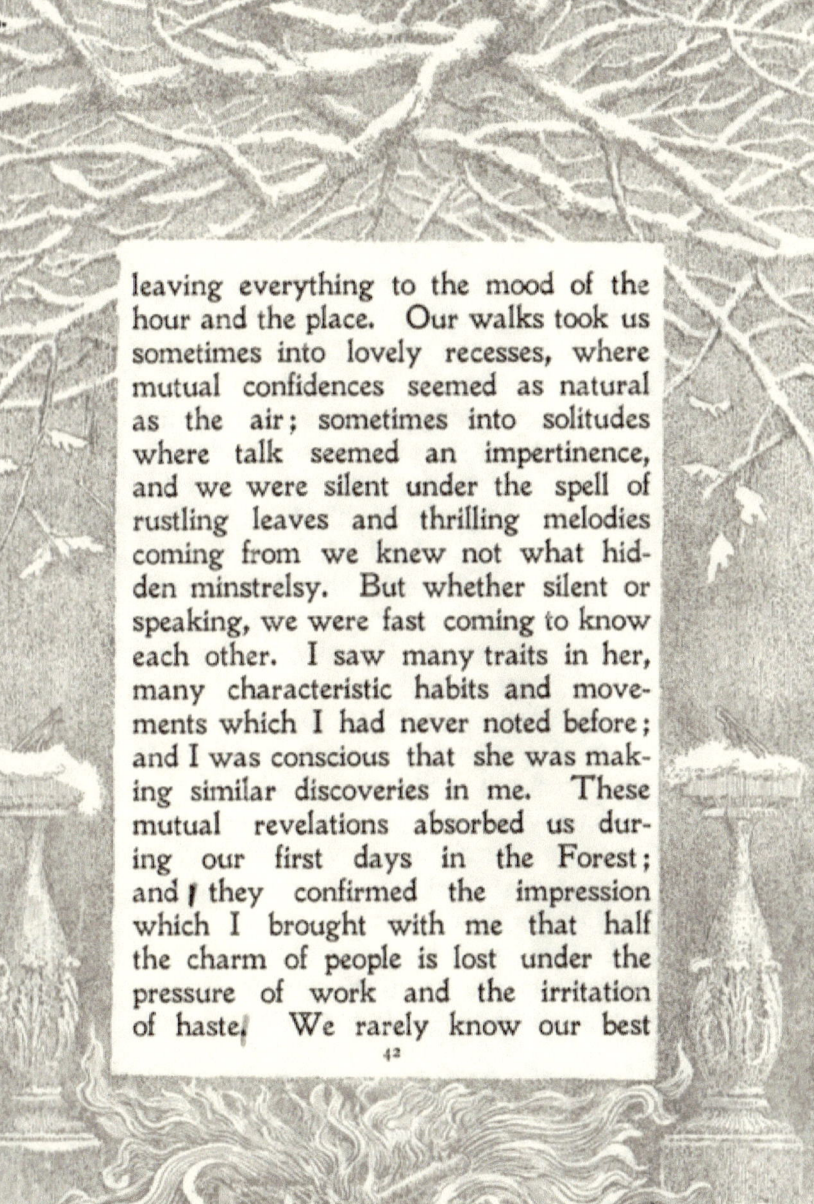

leaving everything to the mood of the hour and the place. Our walks took us sometimes into lovely recesses, where mutual confidences seemed as natural as the air; sometimes into solitudes where talk seemed an impertinence, and we were silent under the spell of rustling leaves and thrilling melodies coming from we knew not what hidden minstrelsy. But whether silent or speaking, we were fast coming to know each other. I saw many traits in her, many characteristic habits and movements which I had never noted before; and I was conscious that she was making similar discoveries in me. These mutual revelations absorbed us during our first days in the Forest; and they confirmed the impression which I brought with me that half the charm of people is lost under the pressure of work and the irritation of haste. We rarely know our best

42

friends on their best side; our vision of their noblest selves is constantly obscured by the mists of preoccupation and weariness.

In Arden, life is pitched on the natural key; nobody is ever hurried; nobody is ever interrupted; nobody carries his work like a pack on his back instead of leaving it behind him as the sun leaves the earth when the day is over and the calm stars shine in the unbroken silence of the sky. Rosalind and I were entirely conscious of the transformation going on within us, and were not slow to submit ourselves to its beneficent influence. We felt that Arden would not put all its resources into our hand until we had shaken off the dust and parted from the fret of the world we had left behind.

In those first inspiring days we went oftenest to the heart of the pines, where the moss grew so deep that our movements were noiseless; where the light fell in subdued and gentle tones among the closely clustered trees; and where no sound ever reached us save the organ music of the great boughs when the wind evoked their sublime harmonies. Many a time, as we have sat silent while the tones of that majestic symphony rose and fell about us, we seemed to become a part of the scene itself; we felt the unfathomed depth of a music produced by no conscious thought, wrought out by no conscious toil, but akin, in its spontaneity and naturalness, with the fragrance of the flower. And with these thrilling notes there came to us the thought of the calm, reposeful, irresistible growth of Nature; never hasting, never at rest; the silent spreading of the tree, the steady burning of the star, the noiseless flow of the river! Was not this sublime unconsciousness of time, this glorious appro-

44

priation of eternity, something we had
missed all our lives, and, in missing
it, had lost our birthright of quiet hours,
calm thought, sweet fellowship, ripen-
ing character? The fever and tumult
of the world we had left were discords
in a strain that had never yielded its
music before.

For nature beats in perfect tune,
And rounds with rhyme her every rune,
Whether she work in land or sea,
Or hide underground her alchemy.
Thou canst not wave thy staff in air,
　Or dip thy paddle in the lake,
But it carves the bow of beauty there,
　And the ripples in rhymes the oars for-
　　sake.

After one of these long, delicious
days in the heart of the pines, Rosalind
slipped her hand in mine as we walked
slowly homeward.

"This is the first day of my life,"
she said.

V

And this our life, exempt from public haunt,
Finds tongues in trees, books in the running brooks,
Sermons in stones, and good in everything

It was one of those entrancing mornings when the earth seems to have been made over under cover of night, and one drinks the first draft of a new experience when he sees it by the light of a new day. Such mornings are not uncommon in Arden, where the nightly dews work a perpetual miracle of freshness. On this particular morning we had strayed long and far, the silence and solitude of the woods luring us hour after hour with unspoken promises to the imagination. We had come at length to a place so secluded, so remote from stir and sound, that one might dream there of the sacredness of ancient oracles and the revels of ancient gods.

Rosalind had gathered wild flowers along the way, and sat at the base of a great tree intently disentangling her treasures. With that figure before me, I thought of nearer and more sacred

49

things than the old woodland gods that might have strayed that way centuries ago; I had no need to recall the vanished times and faiths to interpret the spirit of an hour so far from the commonplaces of human speech, so free from the passing moods of human life. The sweet unconsciousness of that face, bent over the mass of wild flowers, and akin to them in its unspoiled loveliness, was to that hour and place like the illuminated capital in the old missal; a ray of colour which unlocked the dark mystery of the text. When one can see the loveliness of a wild flower, and feel the absorbing charm of its sentiment, one is not far from the kingdom of Nature.

As these fancies chased one another across my mind, lying there at full length on the moss, I, too, seemed to lose all consciousness that I had ever touched life at any point than this, or

that any other hour had ever pressed
its cup of experience to my lips. The
great world of which I was once part
disappeared out of memory like a mist
that recedes into a faint cloud and lies
faint and far on the boundaries of the
day; my own personal life, to which
I had been bound by such a multitude
of gossamer threads that when I tried
to unloose one I seemed to weave a
hundred in its place, seemed to sink
below the surface of consciousness. I
ceased to think, to feel; I was conscious
only of the vast and glorious world of
tree and sky which surrounded me. I
felt a thrill of wonder that I should be
so placed. I had often lain thus under
other trees, but never in such a mood
as this. It was as if I had detached
myself from the hitherto unbroken current of my personal life, and by some
miracle of that marvellous place become
part of the inarticulate life of Nature.

Clouds and trees, dim vistas of shadow and flower-starred space of sunlight, were no longer alien to me; I was akin with the vast and silent movement of things which encompassed me. No new sound came to me, no new sight broke on my vision; but I heard with ears, and I saw with eyes, to which all other sounds and sights had ceased to be. I cannot translate into words the mystery and the thrill of that hour when, for the first time, I gave myself wholly into the keeping of Nature, and she received me as her child. What I felt, what I saw and heard, belong only to that place; outside the Forest of Arden they are incomprehensible. It is enough to say that I had parted with all my limitations, and freed myself from all my bonds of habit and ignorance and prejudice; I was no longer worn and spent with work and emotion and impression; I was no longer prisoned within the iron bars of my own personality. I was as free as the bird; I was as little bound to the past as the cloud that an hour ago was breathed out of the heart of the sea; I was as joyous, as unconscious, as wholly given to the rapture of the hour as if I had come into a world where freedom and joy were an inalienable and universal possession. I did not speculate about the great fleecy clouds that moved like galleons in the ethereal sea above me; I simply felt their celestial beauty, the radiancy of their unchecked movement, the freedom and splendour of the inexhaustible play of life of which they were part. I asked no questions of myself about the great trees that wove the garments of the magical forest about me; I felt the stir of their ancient life, rooted in the centuries that had left no record in that place save the added girth and the discarded leaf; I had no thought

53

about the bird whose note thrilled the
forest save the rapture of pouring out
without measure or thought the joy
that was in me; I felt the vast irresistible movement of life rolling, wave
after wave, out of the unseen seas beyond, obliterating the faint divisions by
which, in this working world, we count
the days of our toil, and making all the
ages one unbroken growth; I felt the
measureless calm, the sublime repose, of
that uninterrupted expansion of form
and beauty, from flower to star and
from bird to cloud; I felt the mighty
impulse of that force which lights the
sun in its track and sets the stars
to mark the boundaries of its way.
Unbroken repose, unlimited growth,
inexhaustible life, measureless force, unsearchable beauty — who shall feel these
things and not know that there are no
words for them! And yet in Arden
they are part of every man's life!

And all the time Rosalind sat weaving her wild flowers into a loose wreath.

"I must not take them from this place," she said, as she bound them about the venerable tree, as one would bind the fancy of the hour to some eternal truth.

"Yesterday," she added, as she sat down again and shook the stray leaves and petals from her lap — "yesterday was the first day of my life: to-day is the second."

It is one of the delights of Arden that one does not need to put his whole thought into words there; half the need of language vanishes when we say only what we mean, and what we say is heard with sympathy and intelligence. Rosalind and I were thinking the same thought. Yesterday we had discovered that an open mind, freedom from work and care and turmoil, make it possible for people to be their true selves and to know each other. To-day we had discovered that nature reveals herself only to the open mind and heart; to all others she is deaf and dumb. The worldling who seeks her never sees so much as the hem of her garment; the egotist, the self-engrossed man, searches in vain for her counsel and consolation; the over-anxious, fretful soul finds her indifferent and incommunicable. We may seek her far and wide, with minds intent upon other things, and she will forever elude us; but on the morning we open our windows with a free mind, she is there to break for us the seal of her treasures, and to pour out the perfume of her flowers. She is cold, remote, inaccessible only so long as we close the doors of our hearts and minds to her. With the drudges and slaves of mere getting and saving she has nothing in common; but with those who hold their souls above the price

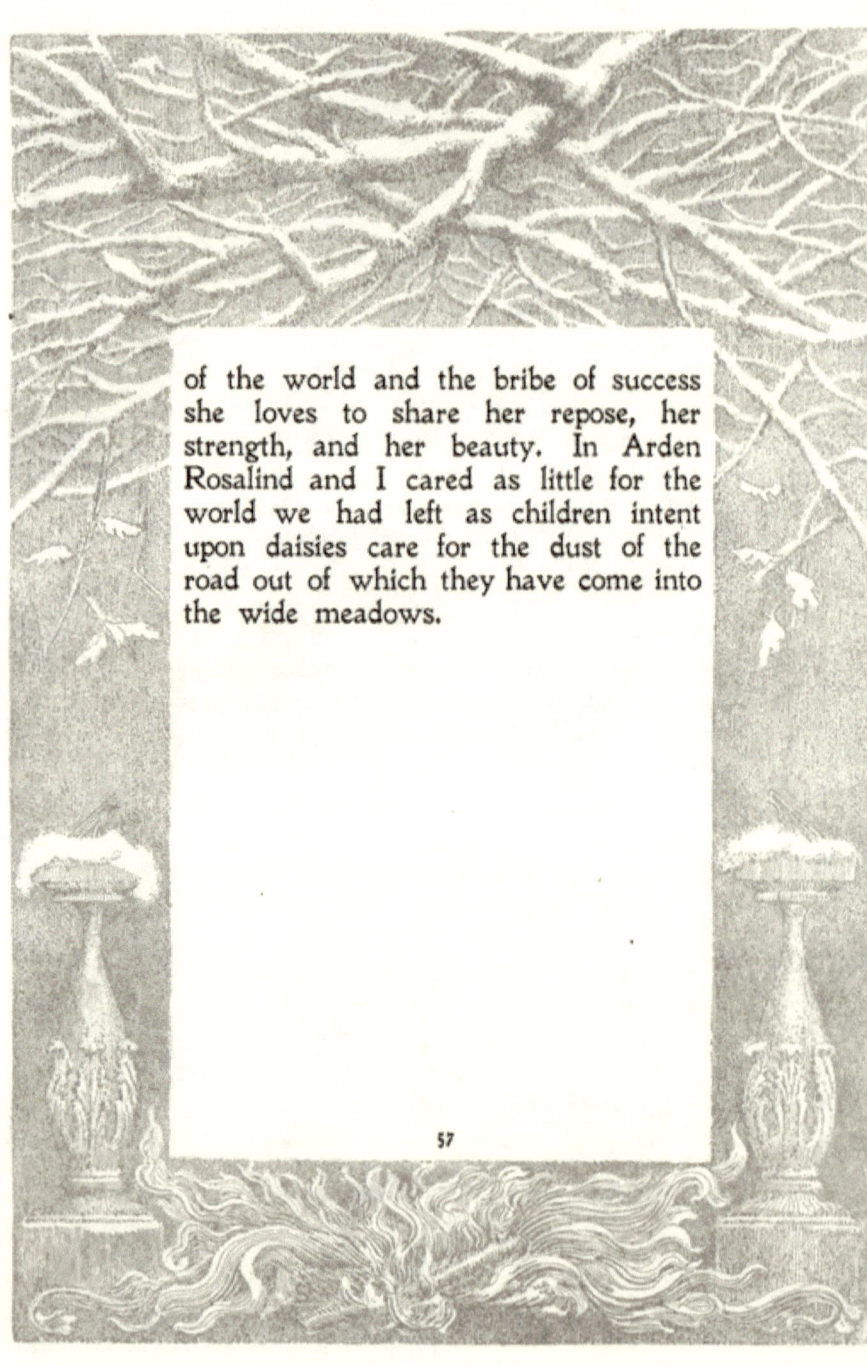

of the world and the bribe of success
she loves to share her repose, her
strength, and her beauty. In Arden
Rosalind and I cared as little for the
world we had left as children intent
upon daisies care for the dust of the
road out of which they have come into
the wide meadows.

VI

Here feel we but the penalty of Adam,
The season's difference, as the icy fang
And churlish chiding of the winter wind,
Which, when it bites and blows upon my body,
Even till I shrink with cold, I smile and say,
This is no flattery: these are counsellors
That feelingly persuade me what I am

If the ideal conditions of life, of which most of us dream, could be realised, the result would be a padded and luxurious existence, well-housed, well-fed, well-dressed, with all the winds of heaven tempered to indolence and cowardice. We are saved from absolute shame by the consciousness that if such a life were possible we should speedily revolt against the comforts that flattered the body while they ignored the soul. In Arden there is no such compromise with our immoral desires to get results without work, to buy without paying for what we receive. Nature keeps no running accounts and suffers no man to get in her debt; she deals with us on the principles of immutable righteousness; she treats us as her equals, and demands from us an equivalent for every gift or grace of sight or sound she bestows. She rejects contemptuously the advances of the weaklings who aspire to become her beneficiaries without having made good their claim by some service or self-denial; she rewards those only who, like herself, find music in the tempest as well as in the summer wind; joy in arduous service as well as in careless ease. A world in which there were no labours to be accomplished, no burdens to be borne, no storms to be endured, would be a world without true joy, honest pleasure, or noble aspiration. It would be a fool's paradise.

The Forest of Arden is not without its changes of weather and season. Rosalind and I had fancied that it was always summer there, and that sunlight reigned from year's end to year's end; if we had been told that storms sometimes overshadowed it, and that the icy fang of winter is felt there, we should have doubted the report. We had a good deal to learn when we first went

to Arden; in fact, we still have a great
deal to learn about this wonderful country, in which so many of the ideals and
standards with which we were once
familiar are reversed. It is one of the
blessed results of living in the Forest
that one is more and more conscious
that he does not know, and more and
more eager to learn. There are no
shams of any sort in Arden, and all
pride in concealing one's ignorance dis-
appears; one's chief concern is to be
known precisely as he is. We were a
little sensitive at first, a little disposed
to be cautious about asking questions
that might reveal our ignorance; but
we speedily lost the false shame we
had brought with us from a world
where men study to conceal, as a means
of protecting, the things that are most
precious to them. When we learned
that in the Forest nobody vulgarises
one's affairs by making them matter

63

of common talk, that all the meannesses of slander and gossip and misinterpretation are unknown, and that charity, courtesy, and honour are the unfailing law of intercourse, we threw down our reserves and experienced the refreshing freedom and sympathy of full knowledge between man and man.

After a long succession of golden days we awoke one morning to the familiar sound of rain on the roof; there was no mistake about it; it was raining in Arden! Rosalind was so incredulous that I could see she doubted if she were awake; and when she had satisfied herself of that fact she began to ask herself whether we had been really in the Forest at all; whether we had not been dreaming in a kind of double consciousness, and had now come to the awakening which should rob us of this golden memory. At last we recognised the fact that we were still in

Arden, and that it was raining. It
was a melancholy awakening, and we
were silent and depressed at breakfast;
for the first time no birds sang, and
no sunlight flickered through the leaves
and brought the day smiling to our
very door. The rain fell steadily, and
when the wind swept through the trees
a sound like a sob went up from the
Forest. After breakfast, for lack of
active occupation, we lighted a few
sticks in the rough fireplace, and found
ourselves gradually drawn into the circle of cheer in the little room. The
great world of Nature was for a moment out of doors, and there seemed
no incongruity in talking about our
own experiences; we recalled the days
in the world we had left behind; we
remembered the faces of our neighbours; we reminded each other of the
incidents of our journey; we retold, in
antiphonal fashion, the story of our

stay in the Forest; we grew eloquent as we described, one after another, the noble persons we had met there; our hearts kindled as we became conscious of the wonderful enrichment and enlargement of life that had come to us; and as the varied splendours of the days and scenes of Arden returned in our memories, the spell of the Forest came upon us, and the mysterious cadence of the rain, falling from leaf to leaf, added another and deeper tone to the harmony of our Forest life. The gloom had gone; we had all the delight of a new experience in our hearts.

"I am glad it rains," Rosalind said, as she gave the fire one of her vigorous stirrings; "I am glad it rains: I don't think we should have realised how lovely it is here if we were not shut in from time to time. One is played upon by so many impressions

that one must escape from them to understand how beautiful they are. And then I'm not sure that even dark days and rain have not something which sunshine and clear skies could not give us." As usual, Rosalind had spoken my thought before I had made it quite clear to myself; I began to feel the peculiar delight of our comfort in the heart of that great forest when the storm was abroad. The monotone of the rain became rhythmic with some ancient, primeval melody, which the woods sang before their solitude had been invaded by the eager feet of men always searching for something which they do not possess. I felt the spell of that mighty life which includes the tempest and the tumult of winds and waves among the myriad voices with which it speaks its marvellous secret. Half the meaning would go out of Nature if no storms ever dimmed the light of stars or vexed the calm of summer seas. It is the infinite variety of Nature which fits response to every need and mood, renews for ever the freshness of contact with her, and holds us by a power of which we never weary because we never exhaust its resources.

"After all, Rosalind," I said, "it was not the storms and the cold which made our old life hard, and gave Nature an unfriendly aspect; it was the things in our human experience which gave tempest and winter a meaning not their own. In a world in which all hearts beat true, and all hands were helpful, there would be no real hardship in Nature. It is the loss, sorrow, weariness, and disappointment of life which give dark days their gloom, and cold its icy edge, and work its bitterness. The real sorrows of life are not of Nature's making; if faithlessness and treachery and every sort of baseness were taken out of human lives, we should find only a healthy and vigorous joy in such hardship as Nature imposes upon us. Upon men of sound, sweet life, she lays only such burdens as strength delights to carry, because in so doing it increases itself."

"That is true," said Rosalind. "The day is dark only when the mind is dark; all weathers are pleasant when the heart is at rest. There are rainy days in Arden, but no gloomy ones; there are probably cold days, but none that chill the soul."

I do not know whether it was Rosalind's smile or the sudden breaking of the sun through the clouds that made the room brilliant; probably it was both. Rosalind opened the lattice, and I saw that the rain had ceased. The drops still hung on every leaf, but the clouds were breaking into great shining masses, and the blue of the sky was of unsearchable purity and depth. The sun poured a flood of light into the heart of the Forest, and suddenly every tiny drop, that a moment ago might have seemed a symbol of sorrow, held the radiant sun on its little disk, and every sphere shone as if a universe of fairy creation had been suddenly breathed into being. And the splendour touched Rosalind also.

VII

. . . Pray you, if you know,
Where in the purlieus of this forest stands
A sheep-cote fenc'd about with olive trees?
.   .   .   .   .   .

The rank of osiers by the murmuring stream
Left on your right hand, brings you to the place.
But at this hour the house doth keep itself

Years ago, when we were planning to build a certain modest little house, Rosalind and I found endless delight in the pleasures of anticipation. By day and by night our talk came back to the home we were to make for ourselves. We discussed plan after plan and found none quite to our mind; we examined critically the houses we visited; we pored over books; we laid the experience of our friends under contribution; and when at last we had agreed upon certain essentials, we called an architect to our aid, and fondly imagined that now the prelude of discussion and delay was over, we should find unalloyed delight in seeing our imaginary home swiftly take form and become a thing of reality. Alas for our hopes! Expense followed fast upon expense and delay upon delay. There were endless troubles with masons and carpenters and plumbers; and when

73

our dream was at last realised, the charm of it had somehow vanished; so much anxiety, care, and vexation had gone into the process of building that the completed structure seemed to be a monument of our toil rather than a refuge from the world.

After this sad experience, Rosalind and I contented ourselves with building castles in Spain; and so great has been our devotion to this occupation that we are already joint owners of immense possessions in that remote and beautiful country. It is a singular circumstance that the dwellers in Arden, almost without exception, are holders of estates in Spain. I have never seen any of these splendid properties; in fact, Rosalind and I have never seen our own castles; but I have heard very full and graphic descriptions of those distant seats. In imagination I have often seen the great piles crown-

ing the crests of wooded hills, whence
noble parks and vast landscapes lay
spread out; I have been thrilled by
the notes of the hunting-horn and dis-
cerned from afar the cavalcade of beautiful women and gallant men winding
its way to the gates of the courtyard;
I have seen splendid banners afloat
from turret and casement; I have seen
lights flashing at night and heard faint
murmurs of music and laughter. Truly
they are fortunate who own castles in
Spain!

In the Forest of Arden there is no
such brave show of battlement and
rampart. In all our rambles we never
came upon a castle or palace; in fact,
so far as I remember, no one ever spoke
of such structures. They seem to have
no place there. Nor is it hard to understand this singular divergence from
the ways of a world whose habits and
standards are continually reversed in

the Forest. In castle and palace, the wealth and splendour of life — everything that gives it grace and beauty to the eye — are treasured within massive walls and protected from the common gaze and touch. Every great park, with its reaches of inviting sward and its groups of noble trees, seems to say to those who pass along the highway: "We are too rare for your using." Every stately palace, with its wonderful paintings and hangings, its sculpture and furnishings, locks its massive gates against the great world without, as if that which it guards were too precious for common eyes. In Arden no one dreams of fencing off a lovely bit of open meadow or a cluster of great trees; private ownership is unknown in the Forest. Those who dwell there are tenants in common of a grander estate than was ever conquered by sword, purchased by gold, or bequeathed by

76

the laws of descent. There are homes for privacy, for the sanctities of love and friendship; but the wealth of life is common to all. Instead of elegant houses, and a meagre, inferior public life, as in the great cities of the world, there are modest homes and a noble common life. If the houses in our cities were simple and homelike in their appointments, and all their treasures of art and beauty were lodged in noble structures, open to every citizen, the world would know something of the habits of those who find in Arden that satisfying thought of life which is denied them among men, — moderation, simplicity, frugality for our private and personal wants; splendid profusion, noble lavishness, beautiful luxury for that common life which now languishes because so few recognise its needs. When will the world learn the real lesson of civilisation, and, for the cheap and ignoble

aspect of modern cities, bring back the
stateliness of Rome and the beauty of
that wonderful city whose poetry and
art were but the voices of her common
life?

The murmuring stream at our door
in Arden whispered to us by day and
by night the sweet secret of the happiness in the Forest, where no man strives
to outshine his neighbour or to encumber
the free and joyous play of his life with
those luxuries which are only another
name for care. Our modest little home
sheltered but did not enslave us; it held
a door open for all the sweet ministries
of affection, but it was barred against
anxiety and care; birds sang at its
flower-embowered windows, and the
fragrance of the beautiful days lingered
there, but no sound from the world of
those that strive and struggle ever en-
tered. We were joyous as children in
a home which protected our bodies,

while it set our spirits at liberty; which
gave us the sweetness of rest and seclusion, while it left us free to use the
ample leisure of the Forest and to drink
deep of its rich and healthful life. Vine-
covered, overshadowed by the pine,
with the olive standing in friendly neigh-
bourhood, our home in Arden seemed
at the same time part of the Forest and
part of ourselves. If it had grown out
of the soil, it could not have fitted into
the landscape with less suggestion of
artifice and construction; indeed, Nature
had furnished all the materials and
when the simple structure was complete
she claimed it again and made it her
own with endless device of moss and
vine. Without, it seemed part of the
Forest; within, it seemed the visible
history of our life there. Friends came
and went through the unlatched door;
morning broke radiant through the lat-
ticed window; the seasons enfolded it

79

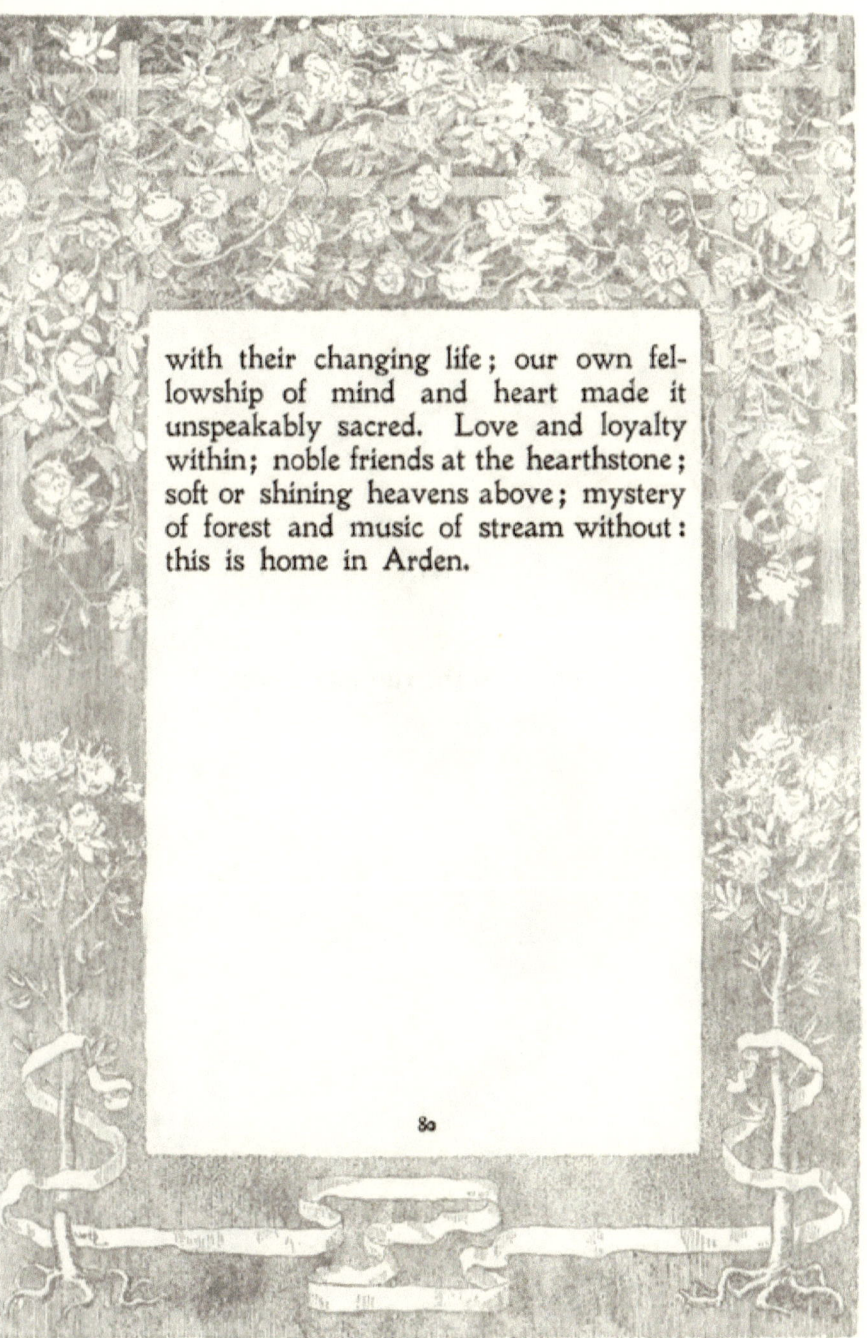

with their changing life; our own fellowship of mind and heart made it
unspeakably sacred. Love and loyalty
within; noble friends at the hearthstone;
soft or shining heavens above; mystery
of forest and music of stream without:
this is home in Arden.

VIII

. . . books in the running brooks

In the days before we went to Arden, Rosalind and I had often wondered what books we should find there, and we had anticipated with the keenest curiosity that in the mere presence or absence of certain books we should discover at last the final principle of criticism, the absolute standard of literary art. Many a time as we sat before the study fire and finished the reading of some volume that had yielded us unmixed delight, we had said to each other that we should surely find it in Arden, and read it again in an atmosphere in which the most delicate and beautiful meanings would become as clear as the exquisite tracery of frost on the study windows. That we should find all the classics there we had not the least doubt ; who could imagine a community of intelligent persons without Homer and Dante and Shakespeare and Wordsworth! How the volumes would be housed we did not try to divine; but that we should find them there we did not think of doubting. Our chief thought was of the principle of selection, long sought after by lovers of books, but never yet found, which we were certain would be easily discovered when we came to look along the shelves of the libraries in Arden. With what delight we anticipated the long days when we should read together again, and amid such novel surroundings, the books we loved! For, although our home contained few luxuries, it had fed the mind; there was not a great soul in literature whose name was not on the shelves of our library, and the companionships of that room made our quiet home more rich in gracious and noble influences than many a palace.

And yet we had been in the Forest several months before we even thought of books; so absorbed were we in the noble life of the place, in the inspiring society about us. There came a morning, however, when, as I looked out into the shadows of the deep woods, I recalled a wonderful line of Dante's that must have come to the poet as he passed through some silent and sombre woodland path. Suddenly I remembered that months had passed since we had opened a book; we whose most inspiring hours had once been those in which we read together from some familiar page. For an instant I felt something akin to remorse; it seemed as if I had been disloyal to friends who had never failed me in any time of need. But as I meditated on this strange forgetfulness of mine, I saw that in Arden books have no place and serve no purpose. Why should one read a translation when the original work lies open and legible before him? Why should one watch the reflections in the shadowy surface of the lake when the heavens shine above him? Why should one linger before the picturesque landscape which art has imperfectly transferred to canvas when the scene, with all its elusive play of light and shade, lies outspread before him? I became conscious that in Arden one lives habitually in the world which books are always striving to portray and interpret; that one sees with his own eyes all that the eyes of the keenest observer have ever seen; that one feels in his own soul all the greatest soul has ever felt. That which in the outer world most men know only by report, in Arden each one knows for himself. The stories of travellers cease to interest us when we are at last within the borders of the strange, far country.

Books are, at the best, faint and imperfect transcriptions of Nature and life; when one comes to see Nature as she is with his own eyes, and to enter into the secrets of life, all transcriptions become inadequate. He who has heard the mysterious and haunting monotone of the sea will never rest content with the noblest harmony in which the composer seeks to blend those deep, elusive tones; he who has sat hour by hour under the spell of the deep woods will feel that spell shorn of its magical power in the noblest verse that ever sought to contain and express it; he who has once looked with clear, unflinching gaze into the depths of human life will find only vague shadows of the mighty realities in the greatest drama and fiction. The eternal struggle of art is to utter these unutterable things; the immortal thirst of the soul will lead it again and again to these ancient fountains, whence it will bring back its handful of water in vessels curiously carven by the hands

of imagination. But no cup of m
making will ever hold all that four
has to give, and to those who
really athirst these golden and be:
fully wrought vessels are insuffici
they must drink of the living str(

In Arden we found these ancient
perennial fountains; and we drank
and long. There was that in the r
tery of the woods which made
poetry seem pale and unreal to
there was that in life, as we saw
the noble souls about us, which r
all records and transcriptions in b
seem cold and superficial. What
had we of verse when the things w
the greatest poets had seen with v
no clearer than ours lay clear and
speakably beautiful before us? V
had fiction or history for us, upon w
the thrilling spell of the deepest hu
living was laid! Rosalind and I
hourly meeting those whose thou

had fed the world for generations, and whose names were on all lips, but they never spoke of the books they had written, the pictures they had painted, the music they had composed. And, strange to say, it was not because of these splendid works that we were drawn to them; it was the quality of their natures, the deep, compelling charm of their minds, which filled us with joy in their companionship. In Arden it is a small matter that Shakespeare has written "Hamlet," or Wordsworth the "Ode on Immortality"; not that which they have accomplished but that which they are in themselves gives these names a lustre in Arden such as shines from no crown of fame in the outer world. Rosalind and I had dreamed that we might meet some of those whose words had been the food of immortal hope to us, but we almost dreaded that nearer acquaintance which

might dispel the illusion of superiority.
How delighted were we to discover that
not only are great souls, really understood, greater than all their works, but
that the works were forgotten and
nothing was remembered but the soul!
Not as those who are fed by the bounty
of the king, but as kings ourselves, were
we received into this noble company.
Were we not born to the same inheri-
tance? Were not Nature and life ours
as truly as they were Shakespeare's and
Wordsworth's? As we sat at rest
under the great arms of the trees, or
roamed at will through the woodland
paths, the one thought that was common to us all was, not how nobly these
scenes had been pictured and spoken,
but how far above all language of art
they were, and how shallow runs the
stream of speech when these mysterious
treasures of feeling and insight are
launched upon it!

IX

. . . every day
Men of great worth resorted
to this forest

The friendship of Nature is matched in Arden with human friendships, as sincere, as void of disguise and flattery, as stimulating and satisfying. There are times when every sensitive person is wounded by misunderstanding of motives, by lack of sympathy, by indifference and coldness; such hours came not infrequently to Rosalind and myself in the old days before we set out for the Forest. We found unfailing consolation and strength in our common faith and purpose, but the frigidity of the atmosphere made us conscious at times of the effort one puts forth to simply sustain the life of his ideals, the charm and sweetness of those secret hopes which feed the soul. What must it be to live among those who are quick to recognise nobility of motive, to conspire with aspiration, to believe in the best and highest in each other? It was to taste such a life as this, to feel the consoling power of mutual faith and the inspiration of a common devotion to the ideals that were dearest to us, that our thoughts turned so often and with such longing to Arden. In such moments we opened with delight certain books which were full of the joy and beauty of the Forest life; books which brought back the dreams that were fading out and touched us afresh with the unsearchable charm and beauty of the Ideal. Surely there could no better fortune befall us than to be able to call these great ministering spirits our friends.

But, strong as was our longing, we were not without misgivings when we first found ourselves in Arden. In this commerce of ideas and hopes, what had we to give in exchange? How could we claim that equality with those we longed to know which is the only basis of friendship? We were unconsciously carrying into the Forest the limitations of our old life, and among all the glad surprises that awaited us there was none so joyful as the discovery that our misgivings vanished as soon as we began to know our neighbours. Neither of us will ever forget the perfect joy of those earliest meetings; a joy so great that we wondered if it could endure. There is nothing so satisfying as quick comprehension of one's hopes, instant sympathy with them, absolute frankness of speech, and the brilliant and stimulating play of mind upon mind where there is complete unconsciousness of self and complete absorption in the idea and the hour. There was something almost intoxicating in those first wonderful talks in Arden; we seemed suddenly not only to be perfectly understood by others, but for the first time to understand ourselves; the horizons of our mental world seemed to be swiftly

95

receding, and new continents of truth were lifted up into the clear light of consciousness. All that was best in us was set free; we were confident where we had been uncertain and doubtful; we were bold where we had been almost cowardly. We spoke our deepest thought frankly; we drew from their hiding-places our noblest dreams of the life we hoped to live and the things we hoped to achieve; we concealed nothing, reserved nothing, evaded nothing; we were desirous above all things that others should know us as we knew ourselves. It was especially restful and refreshing to speak of our failures and weaknesses, of our struggles and defeats; for these experiences of ours were instantly matched by kindred experiences, and in the common sympathy and comprehension a new kind of strength came to us. The humiliation of defeat was shared, we found, by even the greatest; and that which made these noble souls what they were was not freedom from failure and weakness, but steadfast struggle to overcome and achieve. As the life of a new hope filled our hearts, we remembered with a sudden pain the world out of which we had escaped, where every one hides his weakness lest it feed a vulgar curiosity, and conceals his defeats lest they be used to destroy rather than to build him up.

With what delight did we find that in Arden the talk touched only great themes, in a spirit of beautiful candour and unaffected earnestness! To have exchanged the small personal talk from which we had often been unable to escape for this simple, sincere discourse on the things that were of common interest was like exchanging the cloud-enveloped lowland for some sunny mountain slope, where every breath

97

was vital and one mused on half a continent spread out at his feet. | There is no food for the soul but truth, and we were filled with a mighty hunger when we understood for how long a time we had been but half fed. A new strength came to us, and with it an openness of mind and a responsiveness of heart that made life an inexhaustible joy. We were set free from the weariness of old struggles to make ourselves understood; we were no longer perplexed with doubts about the reality of our ideas; we had but to speak the thought that was in us, and to live fearlessly and joyously in the hour that was before us. Frank speaking, absolute candour, that would once have wounded, now only cheered and stimulated; the spirit of entire helpfulness drives out all morbid self-consciousness. Differences no longer embitter when courtesy and faith are universal possessions.

There is nothing more sacred than friendship, and it is impossible to profane it by drawing the veil from its ministries. The charm of a perfectly noble companionship between two souls is as real as the perfume of a flower, and as impossible to convey by word or speech; Nature has made its sanctity inviolable by making it forever impossible of revelation and transference. I cannot translate into any language the delicate charm, the inexhaustible variety, the noble fidelity to truth, the vigour and splendour of thought, the unfailing sympathy, of our Arden friendships; they are a part of the Forest, and one must seek them there. It would vulgarise these fellowships to catalogue the great names, always familiar to us, and yet which gained another and a better familiarity when they ceased to recall famous persons and became associated with those who sat at our hearthstone or gathered about our simple board. Rosalind was sooner at home in this noble company than I: she had far less to learn; but at last I grew into a familiarity with my neighbours which was all the sweeter to me because it registered a change in myself long hoped for, often despaired of, at last accomplished. To be at one with Nature was a joy which made life seem rich beyond all earlier thought; but when to this there was added the fellowship of spirits as true and great as Nature herself, the wine of life overflowed the exquisite cup into which an invisible hand poured it. The days passed like a dream as we strayed together through the woodland paths; sometimes in some deep and shadowy glen silence laid her finger on our lips, and in a common mood we found ourselves drawn together without speech. Often at night, when the magic of the moon has woven all

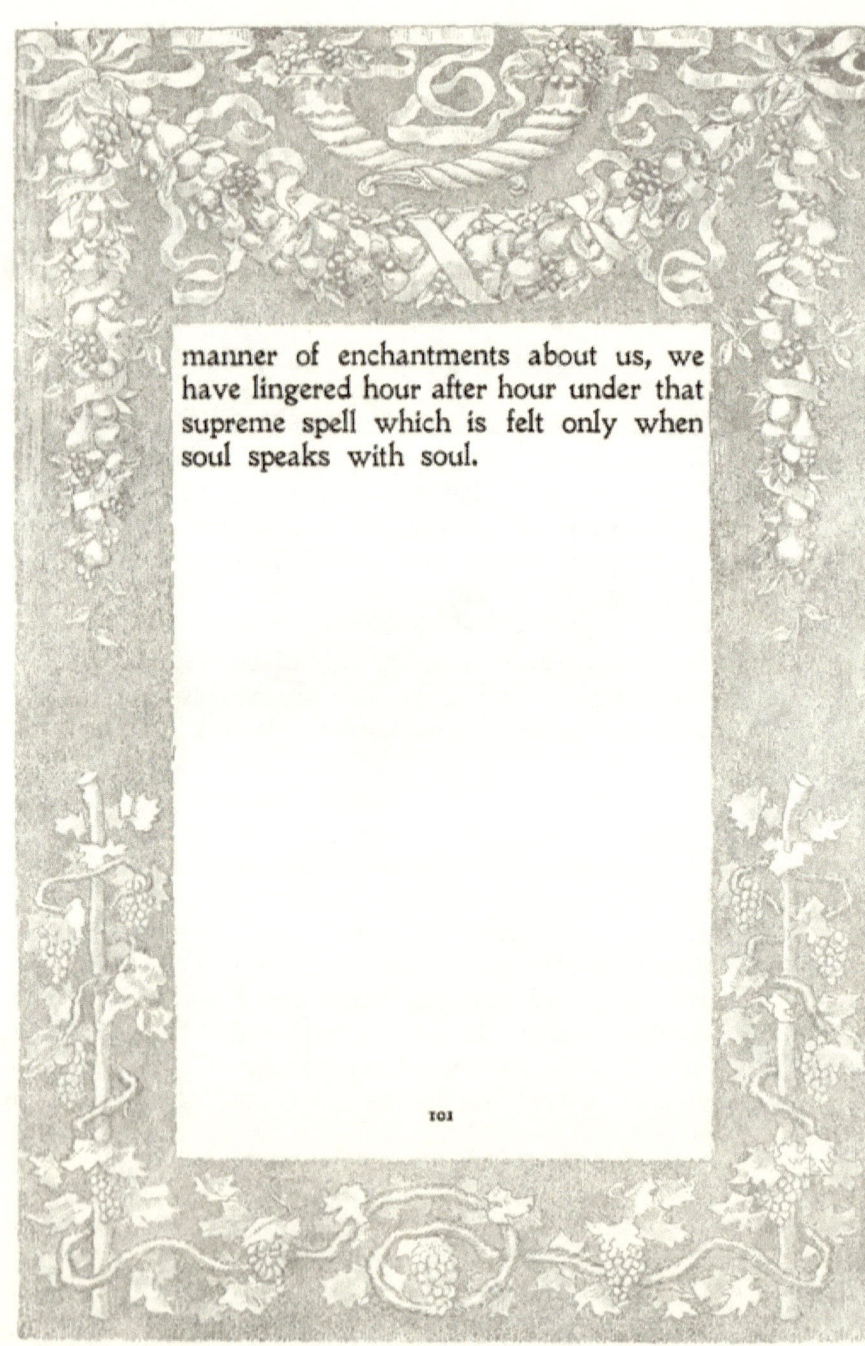

manner of enchantments about us, we
have lingered hour after hour under that
supreme spell which is felt only when
soul speaks with soul.

X

. . . there's no clock in the forest

There were a great many days in Arden when we did absolutely nothing; we awoke without plans; we fell asleep without memories. This was especially true of the earlier part of our stay in the Forest; the stage of intense enjoyment of new-found freedom and repose. There was a kind of rapture in the possession of our days that was new to us; a sense of ownership of time of which we had never so much as dreamed when we lived by the clock. Those tiny ornamental hands on the delicately painted dial were our task-masters, disguised under forms so dainty and fragile that, while we felt their tyranny, we never so much as suspected their share in our servitude. Silent themselves, they issued their commands in tones we dared not disregard; fash-ioned so cunningly, they ruled us as with iron sceptres; moving within so small a circle, they sent us hither and yon on every imaginable service. They severed eternity into minute fragments, and dealt it out to us minute by minute like a cordial given drop by drop to the dying; they marked with relentless exactness the brief periods of our leisure and indicated the hours of our toil. We could not escape from their vigilant and inexorable surveillance; day and night they kept silent record beside us, measuring out the golden light of summer in their tiny balances, and doling out the pittance of winter sunshine with niggardly reluctance. They hastened to the end of our joys, and moved with funereal slowness through the appointed times of our sorrow. They ruled every season, pervaded every day, recorded every hour, and, like misers hoarding a treasure, doled out our birthright of leisure second by second; so that, being rich, we were always impoverished; inheritors of vast fortune, we were put off with a meagre income; born free, we were servants of masters who neither ate nor slept, that they might never for a second surrender their overseership.

There are no clocks in Arden; the sun bestows the day, and no impertinence of men destroys its charm by calculating its value and marking it with a price. The only computers of time are the great trees whose shadows register the unbroken march of light from east to west. Even the days and nights lost that painful distinctness which they had for us when they gave us a constant sense of loss, an incessant apprehension of change and age. Their shining procession leaves no such records in Arden; they come like the waves whose ceaseless flow sings of the boundless sea whence they come. They bring no consciousness of ebbing years and joys and strength; they bring rather a sense of eternal resource and beneficence. In Arden one never feels in haste; there is always time enough and to spare; in fact, the word time is never used in the vernacular of the Forest except when reference is made to the enslaved world without. There were moments at the beginning when we felt a little bewildered by our freedom, and I think Rosalind secretly longed for the familiar tones of the cuckoo clock which had chimed so many years in and out for us in the old days. One must get accustomed even to good fortune, and after one has been confined within the narrow limits of a little plot of earth the possession of a continent confuses and perplexes. But men are born to good fortune if they but knew it, and we were soon reconciled to the possession of inexhaustible wealth. We felt the delight of a sudden exchange of poverty for richness, a swift transition from bondage to freedom. Eternity was ours, and we ceased to divide it into fragments, or to set it off into duties and work. We lived in the consciousness of a vast leisure; a quiet happiness took the place of the old anxiety to always do at the moment the thing that ought to be done; we accepted the days as gifts of joy rather than as bringers of care.

It was delightful to fall asleep lulled by the rustle of the leaves, and to awake, without memory of care or pressure of work, to a day that had brought nothing more discordant into the Forest than the singing of birds. We rose exhilarated and buoyant, and breakfasted merrily under a great oak; sometimes we lingered far on into the morning, yielding ourselves to the spell of the early day when it no longer proses of work and duty, but sings of freedom and ease and the strength that makes a play of life. Often we strayed without plan or purpose, as the winding paths of the Forest led us; happy and care-free as children suddenly let loose in fairyland. We discovered moss-grown paths which led into the very heart of the Forest, and we pressed on silently from one green recess to another until all memory of the sunnier world faded out of mind. Sometimes we emerged suddenly into a wide, brilliant glade; sometimes we came into a sanctuary so overhung with great masses of foliage, so secluded and silent, that we took the rude pile of moss-grown stones we found there as an altar to solitude, and our stillness became part of the universal worship of silence which touched us with a deep and beautiful solemnity. Wherever we strayed the same tranquil leisure enfolded us; day followed day in an order unbroken and peaceful as the unfolding of the flowers and the silent march of the stars. Time

no longer ran like the few sands in a
delicate hour-glass held by a fragile
human hand, but like a majestic river
fed by fathomless seas. The sky, bare
and free from horizon to horizon, was
itself a symbol of eternity, with its
infinite depth of colour, its sublime
serenity, its deep silence broken only
by the flight and songs of birds. These
were at home in that ethereal sphere,
at rest in that boundless space, and
we were not slow to learn the lesson
of their freedom and joy. We gave
ourselves up to the sweetness of that
unmeasured life, without thought of
yesterday or to-morrow; we drank the
cup which to-day held to our lips, and
knew that so long as we were athirst
that draught would not be denied us.

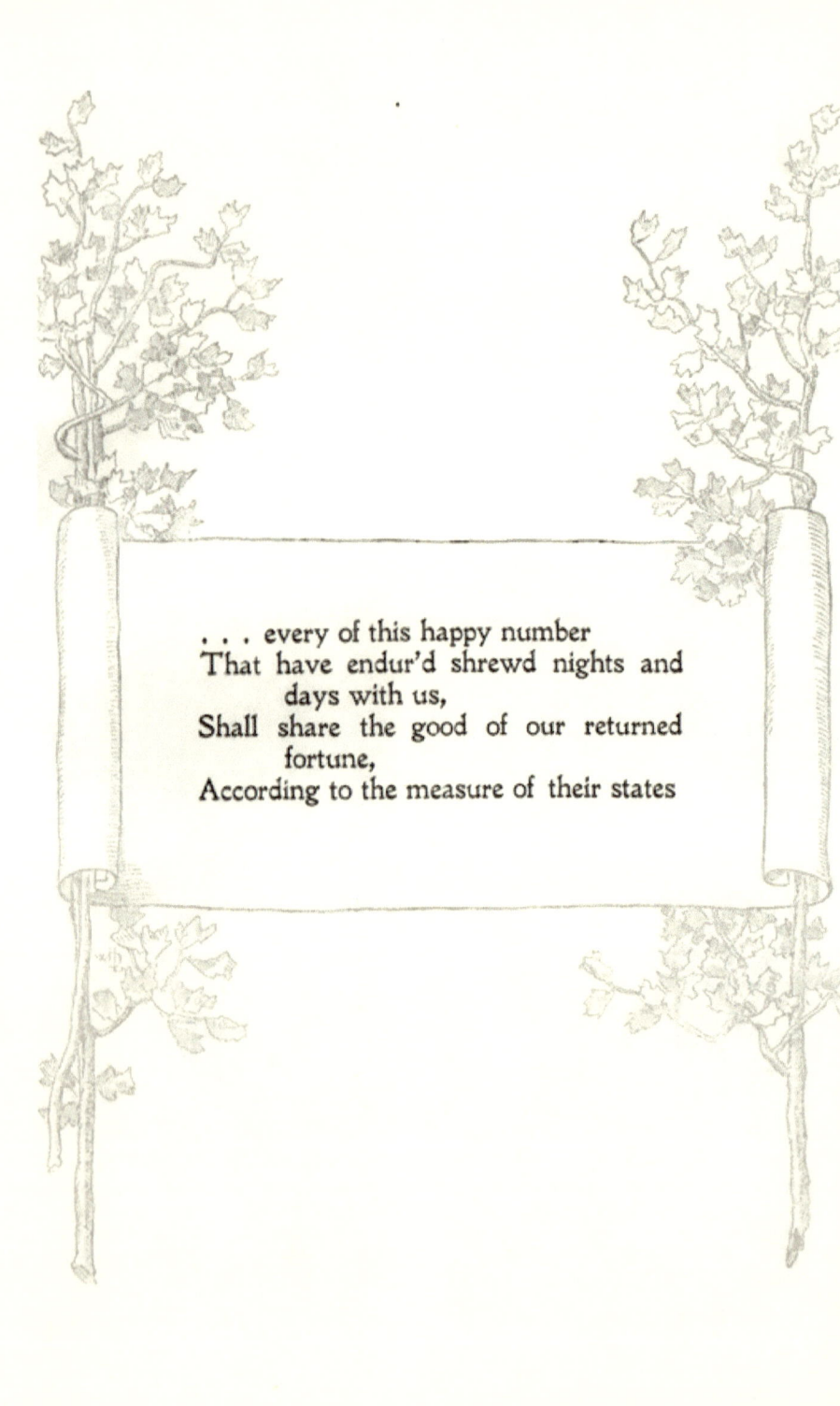

. . . every of this happy number
That have endur'd shrewd nights and
    days with us,
Shall share the good of our returned
    fortune,
According to the measure of their states

There is this great consolation for those who cannot live continually in the Forest of Arden: that, having once proven one's citizenship there, one can return at will. Those who have lived in Arden and have gone back again into the world, are sustained in their loneliness by the knowledge of their fellowship with a nobler community. Aliens though they are, they have yet a country to which they are loyal, not through interest, but through aspiration, imagination, faith, and love. Rosalind and I found the months in Arden all too brief; our life there was one long golden day, whose sunset cast a soft and tender light on our whole past and made it beautiful for us. It is one of the delights of the Forest that only the noblest aspects of life are visible there; or, rather, that the hard and bare details of living, seen in the atmosphere of Arden, yield some truth of character or experience which, like the rose, makes even the rough calyx which encased it beautiful. We had sometimes spoken together of our return to the world we had left, but we put off as long as possible all definite preparations. I am not sure that I should ever have come back if Rosalind had not taken the matter into her own hands. She remembered that there was work to be done which ought not to be longer postponed; that there were duties to be met which ought not to be longer evaded; and when did Rosalind fail to be or to do that which the hour and the experience commanded? We treasured the last days as if the minutes were pure gold; we lingered in talk with our friends as if we should never again hear such spoken words; we loitered in the woods as if the spell of that beautiful

silence would never again touch us. And yet we knew that, once possessed, these things were ours for ever; neither care, nor change, nor time, nor death, could take them from us, for henceforth they were part of ourselves.

We stood again at length on the little porch, covered with dust, and turned the key in the unused lock. I think we were both a little reluctant to enter and begin again the old round of life and work. The house seemed smaller and less homelike, the furniture had lost its freshness, the books on the shelves looked dull and faded. Rosalind ran to a window, opened it, and let in a flood of sunshine. I confess I was beginning to feel a little heartsick, but when the light fell on her I remembered the rainy day in Arden, when the first rays after the storm touched her and dispelled the gloom, and I realised, with a joy too deep for words or tears, that I had brought the best of Arden with me. We talked little during those first days of our home-coming, but we set the house in order, we recalled to the lonely rooms the old associations, and we quietly took up the cares and burdens we had dropped. It was not easy at first, and there were days when we were both heartsore; but we waited and worked and hoped. Our neighbours found us more silent and absorbed than of old, but neither that change nor our absence seemed to have made any impression upon them. Indeed, we even doubted if they knew that we had taken such a journey. Day by day we stepped into the old places and fell into the old habits, until all the broken threads of our life were reunited and we were apparently as much a part of the world as if we had never gone out of it and found a nobler and happier sphere.

But there came to us gradually a clear consciousness that, though we were in the world, we were not of it, nor ever again could be. It was no longer our world; its standards, its thoughts, its pleasures, were not for us. We were not lonely in it; on the contrary, when the first impression of strangeness wore off, we were happier than we had ever been in the old days. Our reputation was no longer in the breath of men; our fortune was no longer at the mercy of rising or falling markets; our plans and hopes were no longer subject to chance and change. We had a possession in the Forest of Arden, and we had friends and dreams there beyond the empire of time and fate. And when we compared the security of our fortunes with the vicissitudes to which the estates of our neighbours were exposed; when we compared our noble-hearted friends with their meaner companionships; when we compared the peaceful serenity of our hearts with their perplexities and anxieties, we were filled with inexpressible sympathy. We no longer pierced them with the arrows of satire and wit because they accepted lower standards and found pleasure in things essentially pleasureless; they had not lived in Arden, and why should we berate them for not possessing that which had never been within their reach? We saw that upon those whom an inscrutable fate has led through the paths of Arden a great and noble duty is laid. They are not to be the scorners and despisers of those whose eyes are holden that they cannot see, and whose ears are stopped that they cannot hear, the vision and the melody of things ideal. They are rather to be eyes to the blind and ears to the deaf. They are to interpret in unshaken trust and patience that which has been revealed to them; servants are they of the Ideal, and their ministry is their exceeding great reward. So long as they see clearly, it is small matter to them that their message is rejected, the mighty consolation which they bring refused; their joy does not hang on acceptance or rejection at the hands of their fellows. The only real losers are those who will not see nor hear. It is not the light-bringer who suffers when the torch is torn from his hands; it is those whose paths he would lighten.

And more and more, as the days went by, Rosalind and I found the life of the Forest stealing into our old home. The old monotony was gone; the old weariness and depression crossed our threshold no more. If work was pressing, we were always looking

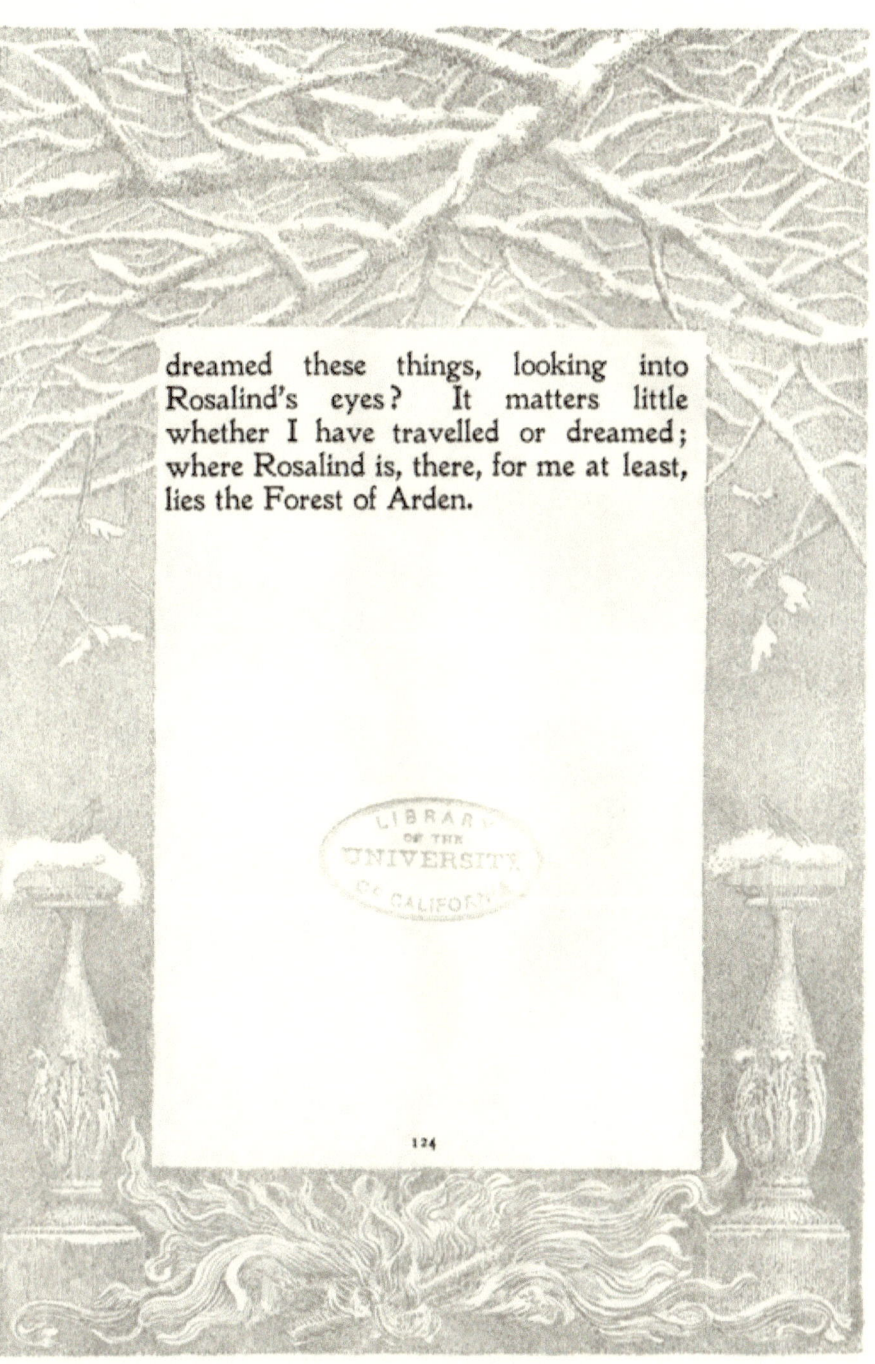

dreamed these things, looking into Rosalind's eyes? It matters little whether I have travelled or dreamed; where Rosalind is, there, for me at least, lies the Forest of Arden.

124